CROC
O'CLOCK

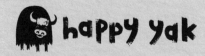

For Kari and Nell.
HUW

For Sam, Han, and Dan.
BEN

Quarto is the authority on a wide range of topics.

Quarto educates, entertains and enriches the lives of our readers—enthusiasts and lovers of hands-on living. www.quartoknows.com

First published in 2021 by Happy Yak, an imprint of The Quarto Group.
26391 Crown Valley Parkway, Suite 220,
Mission Viejo, CA 92691, USA
T: +1 949 380 7510 | F: +1 949 380 7575
www.quartoknows.com

A CIP record for this book is available from the Library of Congress.

ISBN: 978-0-7112-6439-7

Manufactured in Guangdong, China CC082021
9 8 7 6 5 4 3 2 1

MIX
Paper from responsible sources
FSC® C008047

FEEDING TIMES
1:00, 2:00, 3:00, 4:00,
5:00, 6:00, 7:00, 8:00,
9:00, 10:00, 11:00 & 12:00

CROC O'CLOCK

HUW LEWIS JONES AND BEN SANDERS

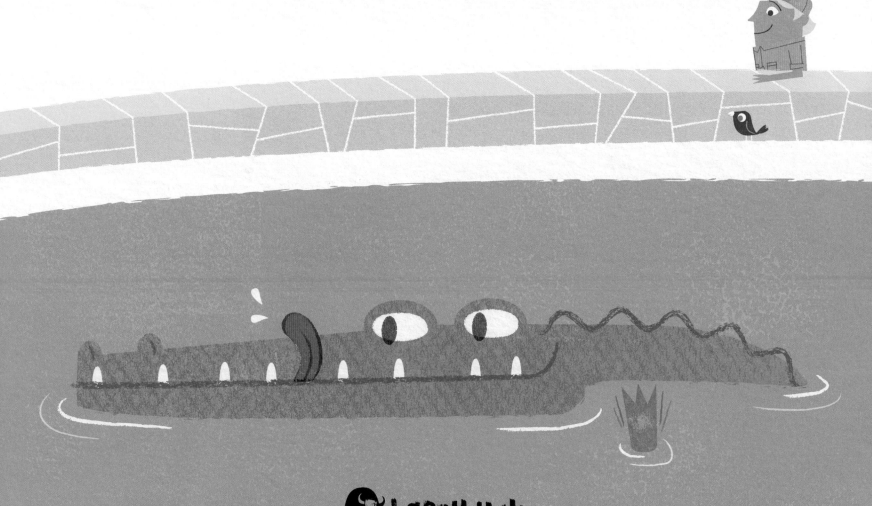

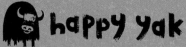
happy yak

HEY, YOU. What are you looking at?

I bet you've come to see me. I'm famous...
the **BIGGEST** croc in the world!

And hour by hour I'm getting even

BIGGER!

IT'S
FEEDING
TIME!

Sing with me!

At one on the zoo clock,
the keepers give to me...

A MOUNTAIN OF
MACARONI!

At two on the zoo clock,
the keepers give to me...

2 CUPS OF TEA!

And a mountain of macaroni!

At three on the zoo clock,
the keepers give to me...

3 FRENCH FRIES!

2 cups of tea

And a mountain of macaroni!

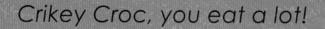

Crikey Croc, you eat a lot!

At four on the zoo clock,
the keepers give to me...

4 PUMPKIN PIES!

3 french fries

2 cups of tea

And a mountain of macaroni!

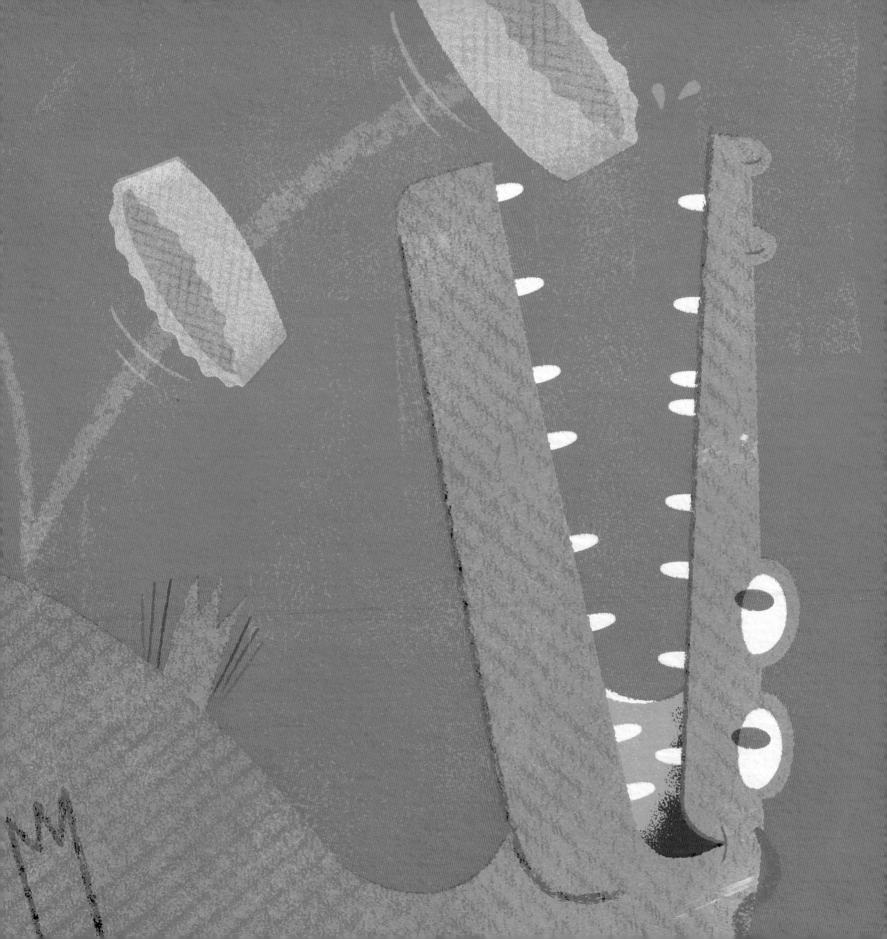

At five on the zoo clock,
the keepers give to me...

5

DONUT RIIINGS!

4 pumpkin pies

3 french fries

2 cups of tea

And a mountain of macaroni!

The clock ticks...
and Croc is still hungry for more!

At six on the zoo clock,
the keepers give to me...

6 TASTY
TOFFEES!

5 DONUT RIIINGS!

4 pumpkin pies

3 french fries

2 cups of tea

And a mountain of macaroni!

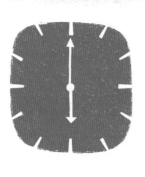

At seven on the zoo clock,
the keepers give to me...

7 CREAMY
COFFEES!

6 tasty toffees

5 DONUT RIIINGS!

4 pumpkin pies

3 french fries

2 cups of tea

And a mountain of macaroni!

At eight on the zoo clock,
the keepers give to me...

8 MIGHTY MILKSHAKES!

7 creamy coffees

6 tasty toffees

5 DONUT RIIINGS!

4 pumpkin pies

3 french fries

2 cups of tea

And a mountain of macaroni!

Oh Croc...
is it time to stop?

At nine on the zoo clock,
the keepers give to me...

9 CHERRY CHEESECAKES!

8 mighty milkshakes

7 creamy coffees

6 tasty toffees

5 DONUT RIIINGS!

4 pumpkin pies

3 french fries

2 cups of tea

And a mountain of macaroni!

At ten on the zoo clock,
the keepers give to me...

10 JUMBO JELLOS!

9 cherry cheesecakes

8 mighty milkshakes

7 creamy coffees

6 tasty toffees

5 DONUT RIIINGS!

4 pumpkin pies

3 french fries

2 cups of tea

And a mountain of macaroni!

At eleven on the zoo clock,
the keepers give to me...

11 LEMON LOLLIES!

10 jumbo jellos

9 cherry cheesecakes

8 mighty milkshakes

7 creamy coffees

6 tasty toffees

5 DONUT RIIINGS!

4 pumpkin pies

3 french fries

2 cups of tea

And a mountain of macaroni!

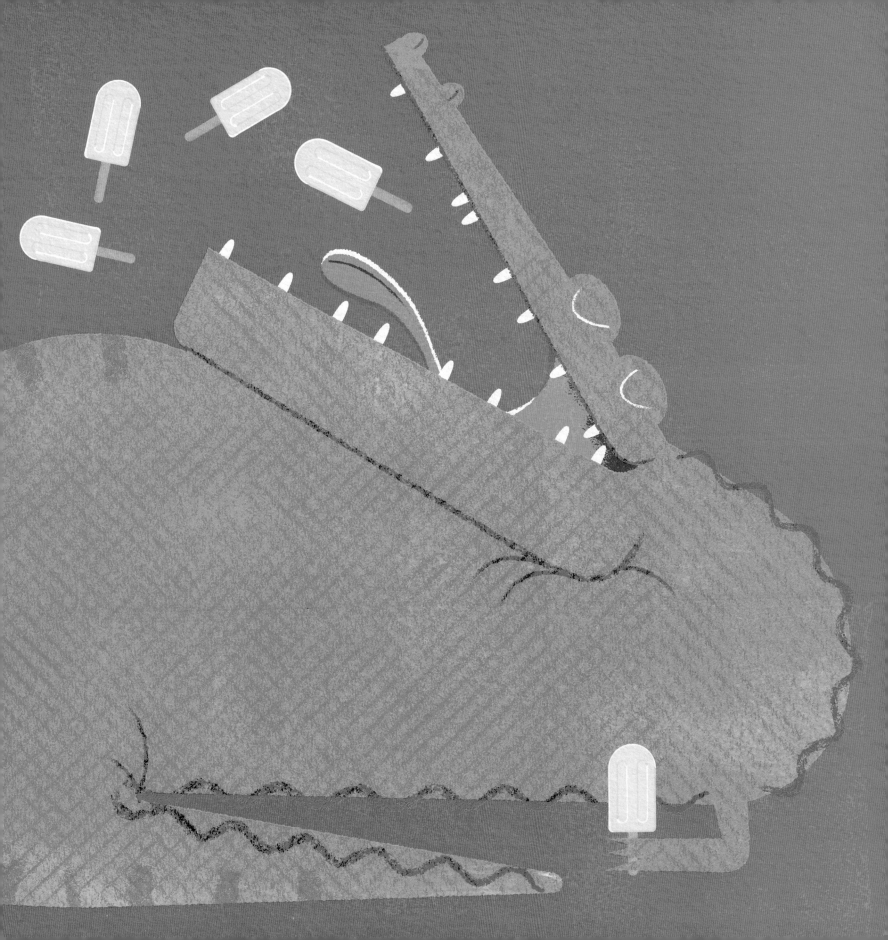

Final verse, Croc— please don't burst!

At twelve on the zoo clock, the keepers give to me...

12 SYRUP SUNDAES!

11 lemon lollies

10 jumbo jellos

9 cherry cheesecakes

8 mighty milkshakes

7 creamy coffees

6 tasty toffees

5 DONUT RIIINGS!

4 pumpkin pies

3 french fries

2 cups of tea

And...

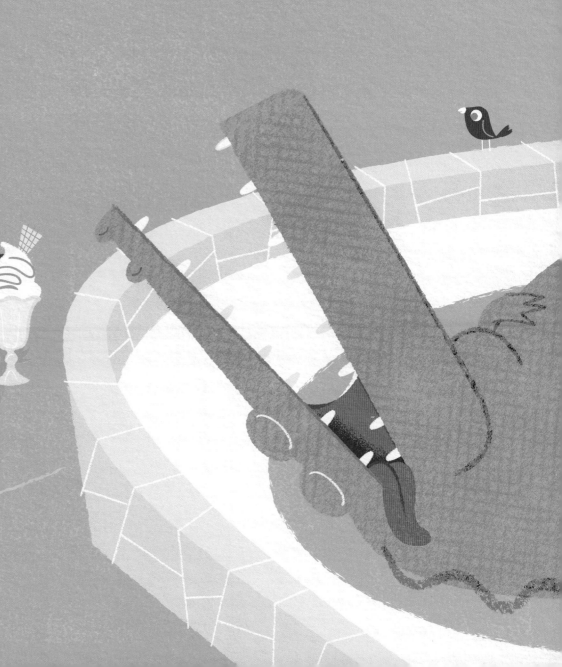

...A PERFECT LITTLE GREEN PEA!

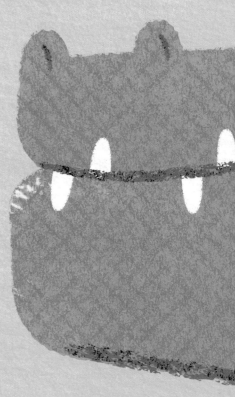

WHAT?!

You have got to be kidding!
If I eat that **PEA** I'll surely…

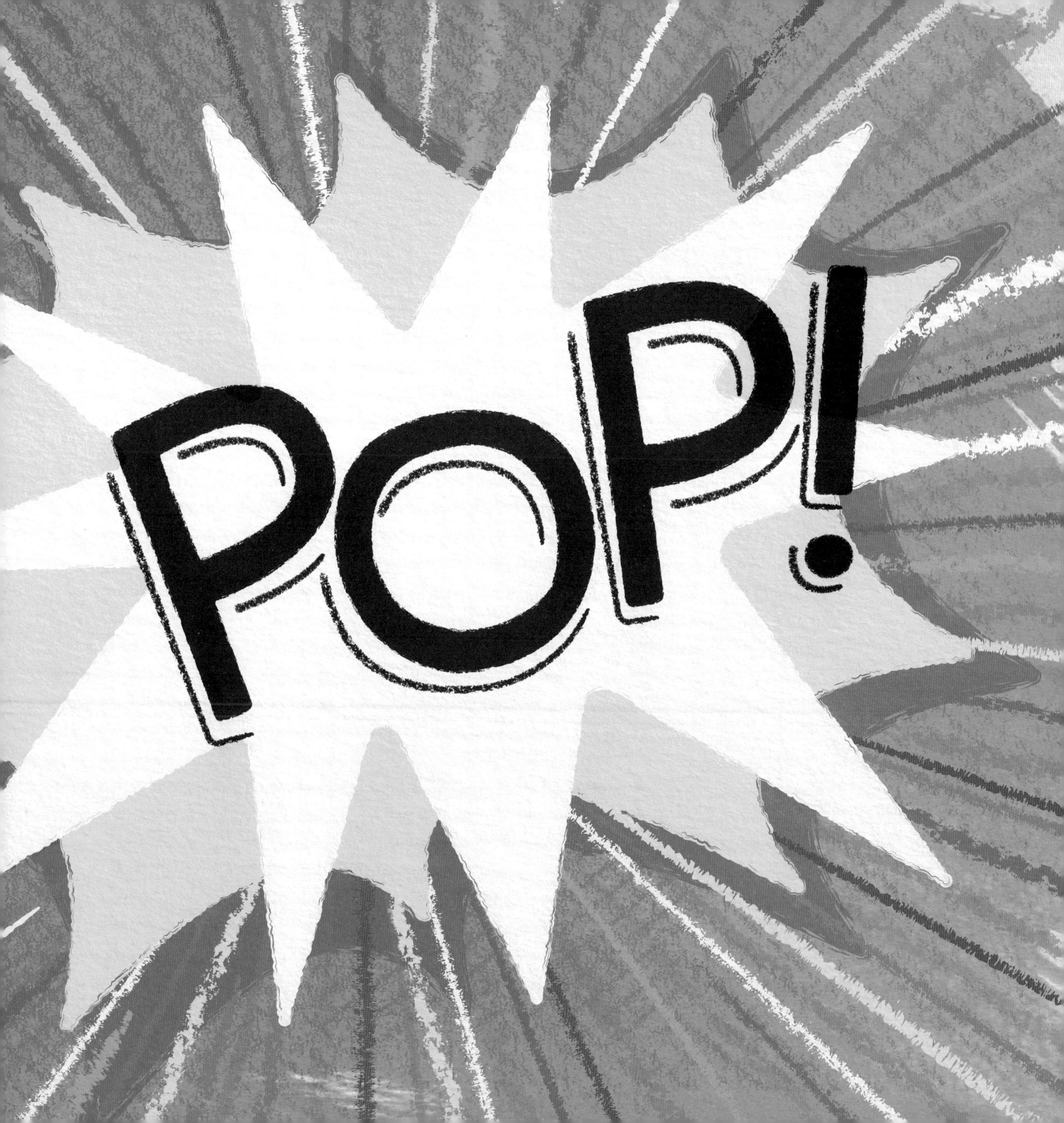
POP!

Nice try, Croc.
But from now on...

IT'S
VEGETABLE
TIME!

ZOO